AUTUMN
PUBLISHING

Published in 2024
First published in the UK by Autumn Publishing
An imprint of Igloo Books Ltd
Cottage Farm, NN6 0BJ, UK
Owned by Bonnier Books
Sveavägen 56, Stockholm, Sweden
www.igloobooks.com

0324 002
2 4 6 8 10 9 7 5 3
ISBN 978-1-83795-031-7

Printed and manufactured in China

CONTENTS

LILO & STITCH

'Ohana means family.

Family means no one gets left behind or forgotten.

Out in space, a creature known as Experiment 626 was hurtling towards Earth in a stolen space cruiser. An alien known as the Grand Councilwoman had offered 626's creator, Jumba, his freedom if he could capture 626 and bring him back. She assigned a nervous agent named Pleakley to go with him.

Meanwhile, on Earth's island of Hawai'i, there lived a little girl named Lilo. She lived with her older sister, Nani, in a small house near the shore. Nani had been called by the school as Lilo had got into trouble. But Lilo didn't wait for her sister, and by the time Nani made it home, a social worker had arrived.

His name was Cobra Bubbles, and he was there to make sure Nani was taking good care of Lilo.

Moments later, once Nani and Cobra were both inside, Lilo appeared. Cobra asked her about life with Nani. Lilo tried to answer the questions the way Nani had taught her, but she got confused and said all the wrong things.

"This did not go well," Cobra said to Nani. "You have three days to change my mind." Then he slammed the front door and left.

Later that night, lights flickered, and the sisters caught sight of a flame streaking across the sky! Lilo thought it was a falling star and quickly ushered Nani out of her room so she could make a wish.

"I need someone to be my friend, someone who won't run away," Lilo said quietly. "Maybe send me an angel… the nicest angel you have."

Lilo & Stitch

The falling star that Lilo thought she saw was actually Experiment 626's spaceship crash-landing on Earth. While exploring, 626 ended up at an animal shelter.

Nani and Lilo arrived at the same shelter the very next day. Nani thought a puppy might help keep Lilo company.

626 was the one Lilo chose. She named him Stitch. The sisters purchased him and took Stitch back home with them.

Later that night, there was a luau. Nani worked as a waitress with a fire dancer named David. At a nearby table, Lilo sat with Stitch while Nani brought them their supper.

Pleakley and Jumba, who'd arrived on Earth, lured Stitch away from the table using a turkey leg. When he was close enough, they pounced! But Stitch chomped on Pleakley's head, which got Nani's attention.

She raced over to help, not realising the tourists were aliens. Immediately after the incident, Nani was fired.

Back at home, Nani told Lilo that it was time to return Stitch to the animal shelter.

"We adopted him!" Lilo shouted. "Dad said *'ohana* means family. Family means…"

"Nobody gets left behind… or forgotten," Nani finished with a sigh.

The following day, Nani went on a job search, and Lilo tried to train Stitch. Unfortunately, every time Nani had an interview, Lilo and Stitch somehow managed to ruin it. By the afternoon, Nani was exhausted and still jobless. All the while, Cobra had been keeping an eye on them.

As they sat on the beach, Lilo and Nani both felt like failures.

Just then, David walked over to them.

"We've been having a bad day," said Lilo.

"I know that there's no better cure for a sour face than a couple of boards and some choice waves," David said.

"I think that's a great idea," Nani said, and soon the family was surfing.

Lilo & Stitch

Stitch rode a wave with Lilo and Nani, but then Jumba appeared! He dragged Stitch underwater, and Stitch pulled Lilo down with him.

Nani saved Lilo but left Stitch behind.

Lilo protested, so David dived down and rescued him.

When they got to shore, Cobra was waiting for them. He felt Nani couldn't handle the responsibility of parenting her little sister. He'd return the next day to take Lilo away.

Nani and Lilo left the beach and headed home. There was a lot they needed to talk about.

15

As the sun went down, Nani tried to explain what would happen the next day. She held Lilo close and sang a Hawai'ian song of goodbye. Nani pulled a flower from her own hair and then one from Lilo's, releasing the two flowers into the night wind. Stitch watched from the deck nearby. He'd never seen anything so beautiful.

Lilo & Stitch

Later that night, Lilo showed Stitch a picture of her family… before the car crash that took her parents away. She tried to ask Stitch about his parents, but he started crawling out of her window.

"'*Ohana* means family," Lilo explained. "Family means nobody gets left behind.

But if you want to leave, you can.

I'll remember you, though.

I remember everyone that leaves."

Stitch did leave and walked into the woods. "I'm lost," Stitch whispered, hoping for a family to rescue him.

Not far away, Jumba and Pleakley got a call from the Grand Councilwoman. Captain Gantu, whose starship Stitch escaped from, was being sent to finish the job.

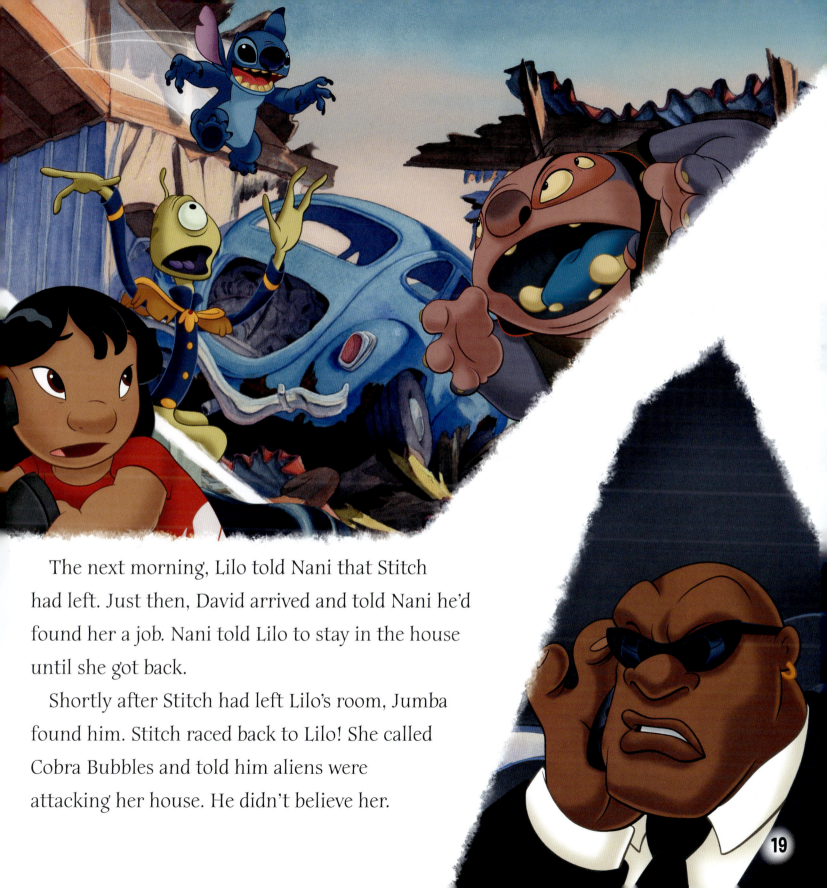

The next morning, Lilo told Nani that Stitch
had left. Just then, David arrived and told Nani he'd
found her a job. Nani told Lilo to stay in the house
until she got back.

Shortly after Stitch had left Lilo's room, Jumba
found him. Stitch raced back to Lilo! She called
Cobra Bubbles and told him aliens were
attacking her house. He didn't believe her.

19

When Nani returned, she found her house destroyed and Cobra Bubbles waiting. He put Lilo in his car to take her away, but Lilo sneaked out of the vehicle.

She raced through the woods and eventually bumped into Stitch. Lilo watched as Stitch transformed into his alien self. Lilo couldn't believe her eyes.

"You're one of them?" she said.

Just then, Captain Gantu popped out of a nearby bush. He captured Stitch – and Lilo, too!

Captain Gantu threw Lilo and Stitch in a glass pod and prepared for take-off. Nani arrived just in time to watch the ship depart.

Somehow, Stitch managed to squeeze through an opening in the glass, but he fell off the ship before he could help Lilo escape.

21

Before Stitch had a chance to explain, Jumba and Pleakley captured him. They admitted there was no way to rescue Lilo.

The aliens tried to get Nani to look on the bright side, but she was devastated.

Stitch walked over to her. "*'Ohana. 'Ohana* means family. Family means…"

"Nobody gets left behind," Nani said.

"Or forgotten," Stitch concluded.

With that, Stitch convinced Jumba and Pleakley to help him rescue Lilo.

Meanwhile, back on Gantu's ship, Lilo looked out and smiled with delight. Stitch waved to her from Jumba's spaceship. She knew he'd come to save her!

Stitch rescued Lilo out of the pod, took a mighty leap and landed her safely on Jumba's ship.

Finally, Jumba's spaceship crash-landed in the ocean. It just so happened that David was out surfing nearby. Lilo asked him if he would give her and the aliens a ride.

As David paddled to shore, the Grand Councilwoman was waiting on the beach. She sentenced Stitch to life in exile, to be served out on Earth. And since Lilo and Nani were Stitch's official caretakers, their family was under the protection of the Galactic Federation.

Lilo, Nani and Stitch were able to stay together as a family… and they had picked up a few new members along the way.

It wasn't a typical family. It was little and broken, but it was still good.

THE DOG SHOW

In the middle of the Pacific Ocean, on the little island of Kaua'i, there lived a young girl named Lilo and her pet, Stitch.

Every weekend, Lilo went to a dance class with the other girls from her town, while Stitch waited patiently outside. But today was different. Today there was another pet waiting outside with Stitch.

When dance class was over, Lilo's classmate Myrtle introduced Lilo and Stitch to her new dog. "Her name is Cashmere. She's a purebred poodle."

Myrtle scowled down at Stitch, who was eating a scoop of ice cream off the pavement. "Breeding is so important when it comes to pets," she said.

Lilo was embarrassed. She tried to ignore the mean things Myrtle said to her and Stitch, but it wasn't easy. "Stitch might not be like other dogs, but he's really smart!" said Lilo.

Just then, Stitch started rolling around in the melted ice cream.

"If Stitch is so smart," Myrtle said, "prove it." She handed Lilo a flyer. "There's a dog show next weekend. Cashmere and I are planning to win, and we'd love to beat you and Stitch."

The Dog Show

Myrtle waved as she and Cashmere strutted away.

Lilo and Stitch both growled, and Lilo crumbled the flyer into a tight ball.

Stitch nuzzled against Lilo. He glanced around to see if anyone could hear him. "Bully," he said.

But Lilo was already smoothing out the dog show flyer. "I'm tired of Myrtle being mean to us. Let's show her and Cashmere what we can do, Stitch!"

Stitch looked at Lilo and then nodded. "For Lilo."

7 Days of Lilo & Stitch Stories

The next weekend, Lilo and Stitch showed up at the dog show. They were ready. At least, they hoped they were. But as the judges led everyone onto the stage, Lilo started to get nervous. She was glad her sister, Nani, had come along to watch.

"Welcome, everyone," a friendly man with a microphone announced. "Let's begin."

The Dog Show

The man gestured to a row of hoops. "Whichever dog can clear these hoops the fastest will win this round. Up first: Lilo and her dog, Stitch!"

Lilo sized up the rings. It would be a tight fit, but she was sure Stitch could zoom though them.

"Go, Stitch. Go!"
Lilo shouted. Stitch took a
deep breath and then
ran towards the rings.
He grabbed the first ring…
and immediately shoved it
in his mouth. He managed
to swallow it whole and then
chomped down the next
four rings. He ran happily
back to Lilo and whispered,
"Clear!"

"No, Stitch," Lilo sighed.
"You were supposed to jump
through the rings."

The Dog Show

Stitch's ears drooped. "Sorry." He burped and then looked back at the shocked audience.

"Well, that's one way to clear rings," the man with the microphone said.

"It's a good thing we have some extra rings for our next contestants!"

Soon the extra rings were set up. Cashmere sped through them and happily bounded back to Myrtle.

"It's okay, Stitch," Lilo said. "We have two events left. We can still win!"
Stitch nodded eagerly.

"On to the next challenge," the man with the microphone shouted as the judges placed three tubes in a zigzag shape on the ground. "In order to complete this event, each dog must run through the three tubes to get to the other side of the course!"

Lilo and Stitch were up first again. "I know you can do this, Stitch," Lilo said. "Just try not to eat anything."

The Dog Show

Stitch licked Lilo playfully and got into position.

"Ready. Set. Go!" the man with the microphone yelled.

Like a bullet, Stitch shot off from the starting line and ran towards the first tunnel. But instead of running inside the tube, the powerful alien smashed through the sides of each tube, running in a straight line from one side of the course to the other.

Stitch crossed the finish line and looked back at the judges proudly. Then he saw Lilo holding her head. Stitch hung his head. He knew he must have done something wrong.

"It's okay. Come here, boy," Lilo called to Stitch.

When Stitch reached her, Lilo said, "I don't think they're going to give us any points for that one, but we still have one event left."

Stitch watched sadly as Cashmere easily navigated the extra tubes. She and Myrtle had so many points, there was no way for Lilo and Stitch to win now.

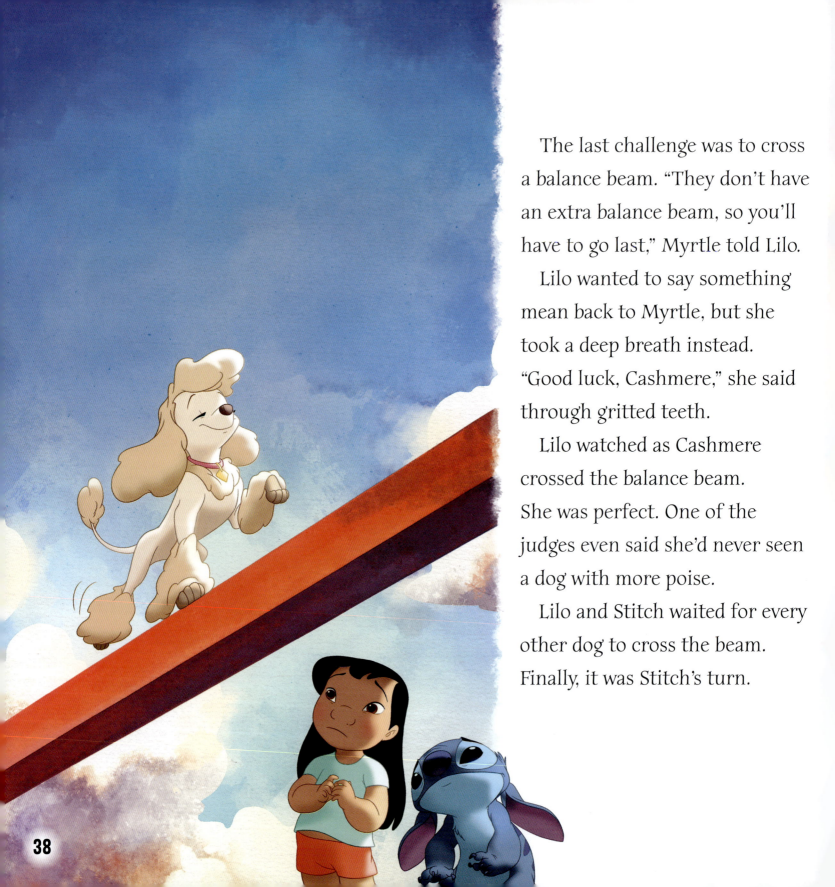

The last challenge was to cross a balance beam. "They don't have an extra balance beam, so you'll have to go last," Myrtle told Lilo.

Lilo wanted to say something mean back to Myrtle, but she took a deep breath instead. "Good luck, Cashmere," she said through gritted teeth.

Lilo watched as Cashmere crossed the balance beam. She was perfect. One of the judges even said she'd never seen a dog with more poise.

Lilo and Stitch waited for every other dog to cross the beam. Finally, it was Stitch's turn.

"Okay, Stitch. Run as fast as you can!" Lilo said.

Stitch nodded and raced towards the beam. One quick hop and he was already halfway across the thin platform. He turned back to smile at Lilo. But as he did, he tripped on the beam. Stitch scratched at the side of the beam. Most dogs would have fallen off the side, but Stitch was no dog. He used his alien arms to keep crawling along the bottom of the beam instead!

The crowd gasped as Stitch dismounted on the other side.

"I think we'd better go," Lilo said quickly.

Lilo ran to Nani and asked her to take them home.

"Don't you want to stay for the results?" Nani asked.

Lilo shook her head. "No. I think we all know who's going to win." She watched as one of the judges rushed to shake Myrtle's hand.

Stitch whimpered beside Lilo. He felt bad for not doing better at the show.

"It's okay, Stitch," Lilo said. "It was my fault. I should have given better instructions."

Nani watched as Lilo hugged Stitch.

That night, Nani tucked Lilo and Stitch into bed. "Don't laugh, but I made you something," she said.

Nani pulled out two large, flat rocks wrapped in shiny tinfoil. "They're supposed to be medals," she said, blushing.

Lilo and Stitch turned the rocks over. On the backs, Nani had written their names and the words 'MOST CREATIVE'. "You did finish all the challenges. You just did them in your own way."

"Thank you, Nani," Lilo said, giving her sister a hug.

"Yes, thanks for Nani," Stitch said, joining the hug. He may not have won the dog show, but he had something even better… a family that loved him no matter what!

HOLIDAY MISCHIEF WITH STITCH

"Ready or not, here I come!" Lilo shouted.

It was a warm December morning in Hawai'i, and Lilo and Stitch were playing hide-and-seek.

Stitch was very good at hiding!

"Surprise!" Stitch shouted as he jumped out of a box.

Lilo laughed. "Stitch! Those are for Christmas."

"Christmas?" Stitch was confused. He had never celebrated Christmas before.

"The end of the year is full of festivities here on Earth," Lilo explained. "It's a time when everyone comes together to spread peace and joy. Come on! I'll show you."

Lilo took Stitch downtown to the dance studio. Lilo's sister, Nani, was
helping the dancers prepare for a big holiday party.

Some dancers were hanging colourful lights.

Other dancers were weaving tinsel into leis for guests to wear.

Holiday Mischief With Stitch

"During the holidays we have lots of big parties," Lilo said. "Friends from all over the island come to celebrate. And they bring lots of food." Stitch liked the sound of that! He wanted to help get ready for the party. He grabbed a string of lights and began running around.

"Stitch, slow down!" Lilo called. But Stitch did not slow down. The lights got tangled up in Nani's banner and tipped over the poinsettias.

Stitch tripped on a lei and fell, rolling himself into a knot of fur and Christmas lights.

Stitch snarled and began pulling at the lights. But the harder Stitch pulled, the more of a mess he made.

Lilo sighed and helped Stitch escape from the tangle of lights.

"Don't be naughty, Stitch!" Lilo said.

"That's not the way we celebrate *'ohana*, our family. Plus, if you're naughty, you won't get any presents."

"Presents?" Stitch asked.

Lilo told Stitch the story of old Saint Nick, who delivers presents to good children at Christmas. To help remind Stitch to be good, she wrote 'naughty' and 'nice' on opposite sides of his hat.

Stitch felt bad for ruining the studio's decorations.

He apologised and helped Lilo, Nani and the dancers clean up the mess.

Lilo decided to teach Stitch about other holiday traditions. She took him to a friend's house, where they saw a big menorah. Lilo told Stitch that the menorah is a symbol of Hanukkah.

The holiday lasts for eight days, and every night, a new candle is lit in remembrance.

"Some families get together for fun traditions like spinning the dreidel and eating potato pancakes called latkes!"

"Eight days?" Stitch asked. That long holiday sounded like a lot of fun. Stitch decided to spin the dreidel. It twirled and it twirled until...

The dreidel spiralled off the table and the latkes fell, too!

"Be careful, Stitch!" Lilo yelled. "Remember what I said about being naughty?"

53

Stitch put the dreidel and latkes back on the table. "Don't forget that the holidays are all about celebrating *'ohana*," Lilo told Stitch. "If you promise to be nice, I'll teach you about one more holiday tradition."

Stitch nodded. He would be on his best behaviour!

Holiday Mischief With Stitch

Lilo took Stitch to their friend Mr Bubbles' house. Mr Bubbles had just finished baking a batch of cookies.

Stitch's stomach rumbled, but he waited patiently for Lilo to get a cookie first.

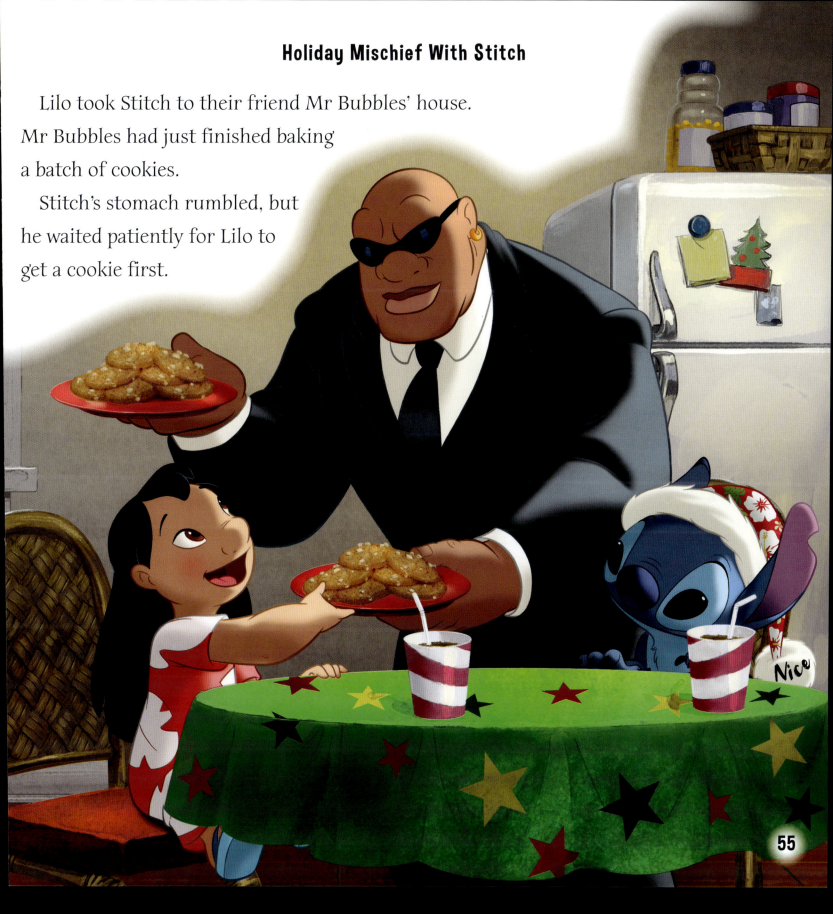

Mr Bubbles explained that during the last week of the year his family celebrated Kwanzaa.

"My favourite Kwanzaa tradition is when the whole family drinks from the unity cup," Mr Bubbles said. "Well, that and baking my grandmother's famous macadamia nut cookies."

Holiday Mischief With Stitch

"The unity cup honours family that is no longer with us,"
Mr Bubbles said. "And so do my grandmother's cookies."
Stitch helped himself to a second cookie. And a third.
He reached for a fourth.

Stitch was about to stuff all the cookies in his mouth. But then he heard Lilo's voice in his head: the holidays are all about celebrating *'ohana*!

Stitch wanted Lilo to be proud of him. He quietly put the cookies back.

Lilo smiled. She was glad Stitch had chosen to be nice.

"Why don't I give you two a box of cookies for the road?" Mr Bubbles said.

"Yes!" Stitch cheered.

Lilo and Stitch shared the delicious cookies as they walked home.

Holiday Mischief With Stitch

At home, Nani had everything ready to decorate the Christmas tree. Stitch ran lights all the way to the top of it. Lilo played Christmas music on her record player. Nani hung ornaments on every branch.

This was Lilo's favourite Christmas tradition: spending time with her family.

RIDE THE WAVES

One sunny afternoon, Lilo's older sister, Nani, was at the beach with David. They were checking out a poster for a surfing competition when they noticed Stitch getting into trouble.

Nani and David rushed right over.

"Guys, you can't just dash all over the beach causing trouble!" said Nani.

"How about you two put your energy to good use?" said David. "The Kaua'i Kurl Surf Competition is next Saturday. Nani and I are entering. You should enter, too!"

Lilo wasn't sure. She loved the beach and liked to swim, but getting on a surfboard without her sister made her nervous.

Stitch felt the same and shook his own head so fast he almost fell backwards!

"Come on," said Nani. "I'll teach you both how to surf like champions!"

Lilo hadn't thought of it that way. If surfing meant more time with Nani and Stitch… Lilo would do it for *'ohana*, the family!

"Okay, we're in!" said Lilo, and everyone high-fived.

Nani took Lilo and Stitch to the surf shop so they could rent a board. While looking for the perfect one, they saw Myrtle, Lilo's classmate.

"Hey, Lilo," said Myrtle. "I didn't know you were a surfer."

"I didn't know you were a surfer, either," said Lilo, eyeing the bar of surf wax Myrtle held. "Anyway, my sister, Nani, is going to help me surf like a champion for the competition next weekend."

"I've entered the competition, too... and I'm going to win!" said Myrtle.

"Don't worry, Lilo," said Nani as they left the surf shop. "Surfing isn't about winning. It's about having fun, right?"

Lilo wasn't so sure. She was beginning to wonder why she had agreed to enter the competition in the first place. Oh, right... for *ohana*.

Ride the Waves

Lilo felt better once Myrtle was gone and she was back on the beach.

Stitch ran straight for the ocean, but Nani stopped him. She had Stitch and Lilo place the board on the sand.

"You are going to have to get out to the waves all by yourself," Nani said.

"First lie down flat on your belly," she instructed.

"Now paddle with your arms. Imagine a big wave is coming, and push up quickly," said Nani.

"Plant both feet on the board at the same time, and… there!" cried Nani. That was good, Lilo!"

Maybe I can do this, thought Lilo.

Ride the Waves

"You're supposed to do that in the water, I think," boomed a big voice, followed by some laughter. It was their friend Mr Bubbles!

"Nani is teaching us on the sand first," said Lilo. "But I think we're ready to try it out there!" Lilo pointed to the waves, and Stitch nodded.

"Okay, then," said Nani, smiling. "Remember, if you get knocked down, just get right back up again."

Lilo and Stitch picked up the surfboard and headed for the water.

But before they could even get onto their board, a wave sent them tumbling!

Lilo remembered what Nani had said, and together with Stitch, she got right back up again. This time they made it onto the surfboard and through the ocean blue waves.

Lilo and Stitch paddled out. Nani followed on her own board.

The whole family was together on the water!

Lilo and Stitch practised hard that day, but they still couldn't stand on their board.

For the rest of the week, Lilo and Stitch focused on strength training and practising their surfing technique.

By Friday, Lilo and Stitch were riding the waves! Lilo's body felt strong and steady.

73

Finally, it was the big day.

"I'm nervous," Lilo said.

"Lilo, you've practised all week," Nani replied, "and your hard work will pay off. Just do your best. I'll be right out there with you… We'll show the competition what the Pelekai sisters can do!"

"And Stitch?" said Stitch.

"Yes, of course!" said Nani. "Stitch, too! Let's go!"

Ride the Waves

At the beach, they saw many of the competitors lined up with their surfboards, their eyes fixed on the waves.

"Intimidated?" said Myrtle, who was waiting on the beach, too. "You should be. Get ready to wave goodbye to first place!"

But Lilo didn't let Myrtle get to her. Instead, she remembered what Nani had said. She had practised. She was ready.

The official blew the whistle.

Everyone ran to the waves!

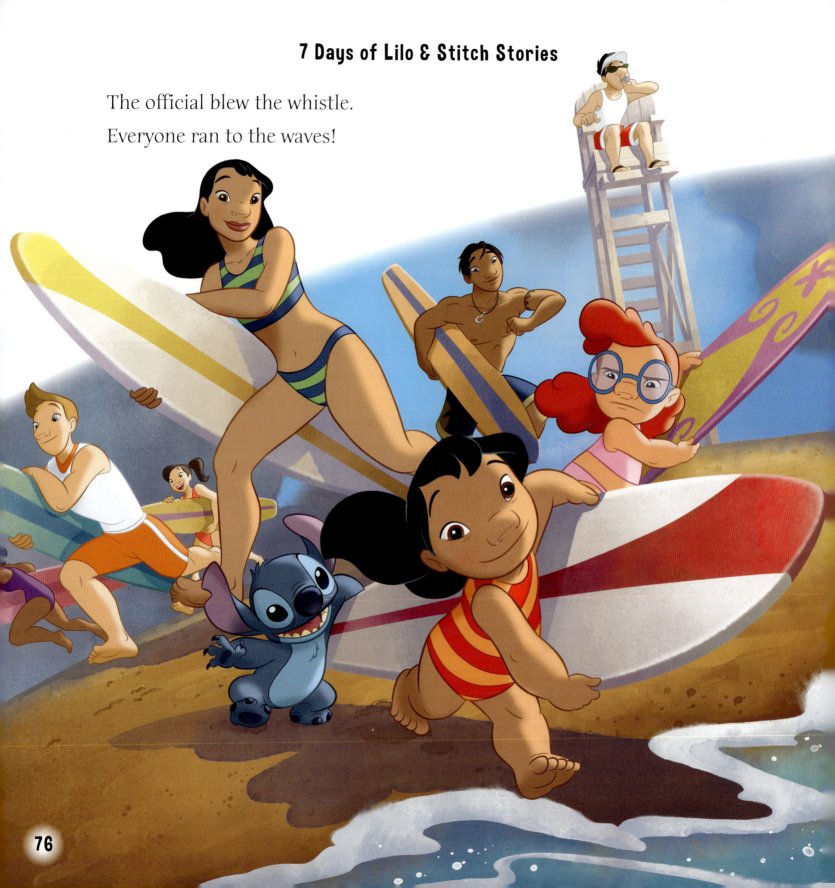

Together, Lilo and Stitch paddled out, jumped up and stuck the landing with all four of their feet.

"Go, Lilo and Stitch! Go!" shouted Nani and David across the waves.

Myrtle hit a wave the wrong way and totally wiped out. Instead of getting back on her board, Myrtle dragged herself to shore.

7 Days of Lilo & Stitch Stories

Lilo and Stitch were riding high! It felt great to be out on the ocean, their faces against the wind, surfing so well.

Lilo glanced at the judges on the beach.

We'll show them what we can do, she thought.

Ride the Waves

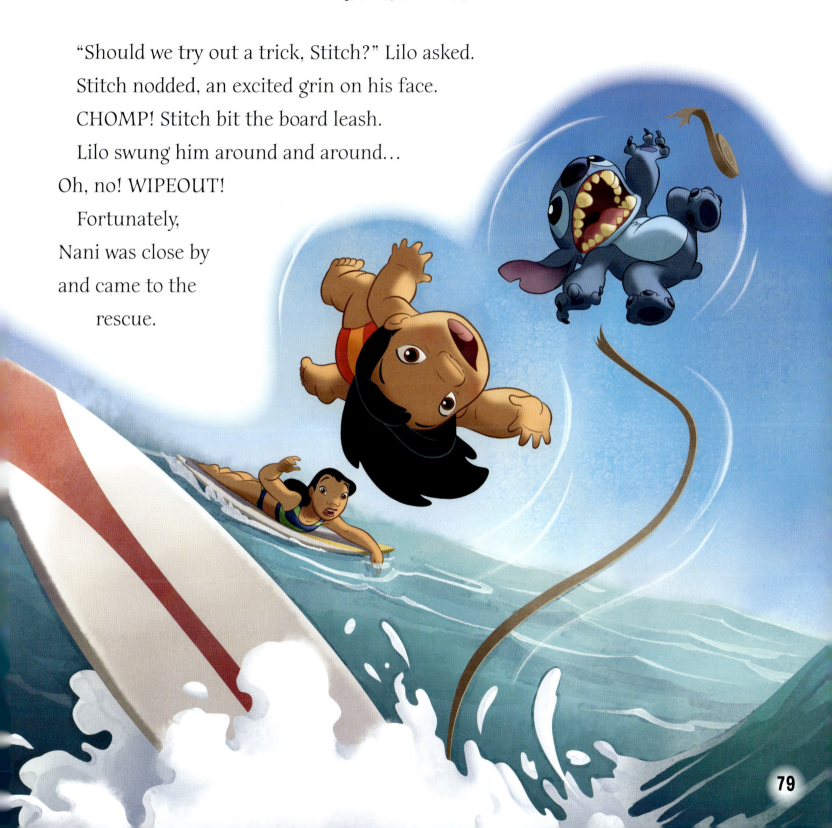

"Should we try out a trick, Stitch?" Lilo asked.

Stitch nodded, an excited grin on his face.

CHOMP! Stitch bit the board leash.

Lilo swung him around and around…

Oh, no! WIPEOUT!

Fortunately, Nani was close by and came to the rescue.

"Lilo, Stitch! Are you okay?" asked Nani as she pulled them onto her surfboard.

Lilo coughed up some seawater. "I think so, but our board is gone. We'll never win now!" she moaned.

"You don't have to show off to prove that you're strong," said Nani. "And the most important thing isn't winning, right? It's—"

"Getting right back up again when you get knocked down?" finished Lilo.

"Yes. Now let's show them what we can do… together!" said Nani.

Soon a massive wave came. It was ten times the size of Lilo and twenty times the size of Stitch!

"Imagine your heart and the wave's heart are one and the same," Nani said as the wave came closer. The words helped Lilo feel braver.

Lilo hopped up onto Nani's shoulders, and then Stitch scrambled up onto Lilo's shoulders. Together, they surfed all the way to shore.

Lilo, Stitch and Nani won the award for 'best teamwork'. The whole family, *ohana*, did it together!

The special prize was a trophy and a new surfboard.

"For me?" Lilo asked.

"For you, Sister," said Nani. "You deserve it. And now we can keep practising... for next year's surfing competition!"

A VALENTINE FOR STITCH

One sunny Valentine's Day morning, Lilo and Stitch were finishing a batch of homemade cards.

"This one needs more glitter," Lilo said.

"Right!" said Stitch.

Stitch didn't know much about Valentine's Day, but he was happy to celebrate a holiday where people gave gifts to each other.

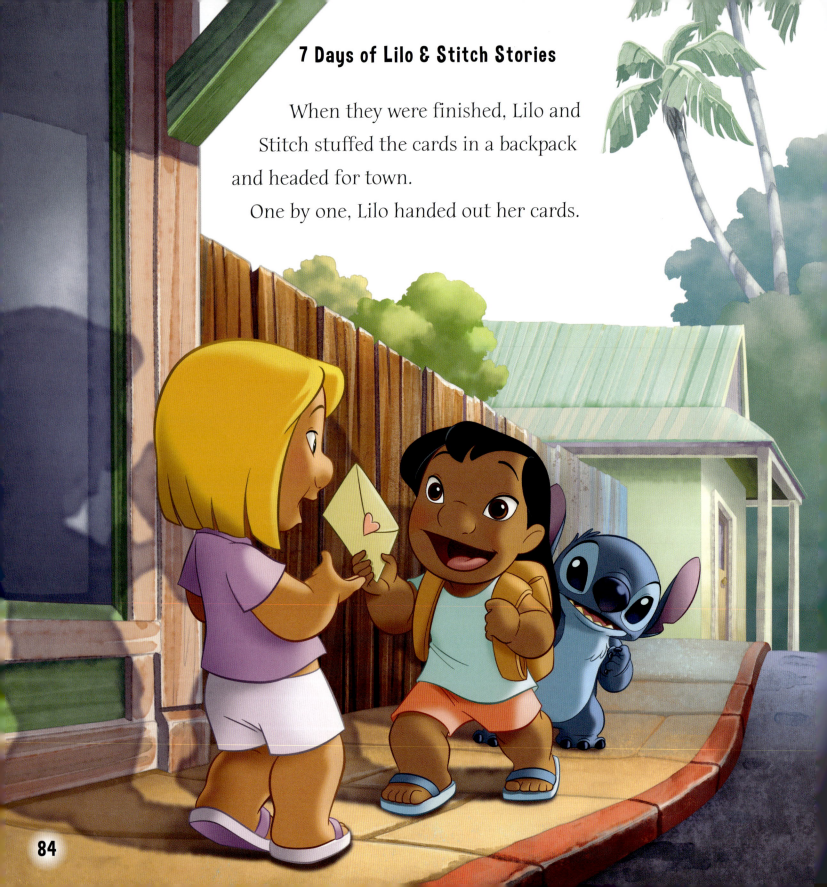

When they were finished, Lilo and Stitch stuffed the cards in a backpack and headed for town.

One by one, Lilo handed out her cards.

A Valentine for Stitch

Stitch watched Lilo and the people in town share their valentines cards.

Lilo had told Stitch that when you gave a present to someone on Valentine's Day, it meant that they were your valentine. It seemed like everyone had a friend to give a gift to.

Stitch wished he had someone to be his valentine.

While walking with Lilo through town, Stitch noticed a winged baby with a bow and arrow hanging in a shop window.

"That's Cupid," said Lilo. "He's a little angel who spreads love on Valentine's Day."

A Valentine for Stitch

"Angel?" said Stitch.

He was suddenly reminded of his friend Angel.

Stitch and Angel had a lot in common. They were both scientific experiments that came to Hawai'i from outer space. But unlike Stitch, Angel loved to sing.

"Can Angel be Stitch's valentine?" asked Stitch.

"Of course!" said Lilo. "Where is she?"

A Valentine for Stitch

Stitch didn't know. He had not seen Angel in a long time.
She preferred to hang out in the rainforest.

"Well…" said Lilo, "let's go find her!"

"Yes!" said Stitch. He dashed for the trees.

Lilo ran after him and hollered,
"Wait for me!"

They searched deep into the rainforest but had no luck
finding Angel. Until…

"Look!" said Lilo. "Angel's right there!"

A Valentine for Stitch

Stitch rushed over to say hello. But it was only an Angel-shaped cluster of rocks and leaves.

As the day wore on, they began to lose hope.

"I think we should head back," said Lilo. Stitch sighed. Now he would never have a valentine!

Just then, Stitch heard beautiful singing from across the canyon. Lilo took binoculars out of her backpack and scanned the area. "There she is!" she cried.

A Valentine for Stitch

Lilo and Stitch hurried towards the pink alien.

"Angel!" Stitch shouted.

Angel gave a frightened yelp. But when she saw Stitch's big toothy grin, she smiled.

"Happy Valentine's Day!" said Stitch.

Angel looked confused. She didn't know what Valentine's Day was.

"Try explaining it to her," whispered Lilo.

Stitch gulped. "Ah… oh… um…"

He couldn't find the right words to say, but he remembered what he had seen others do for their valentines back in town.

Stitch decided he would show Angel the meaning of Valentine's Day.

He snatched some flowers and handed them to Angel. But the pollen made her sneeze.

"Ah-CHOO!"

Then Stitch improvised a song for Angel.

"JAALBA JAALBA BOOTIFA!"

But he sang too loud and out of tune.

Stitch thought hard about what to try next.

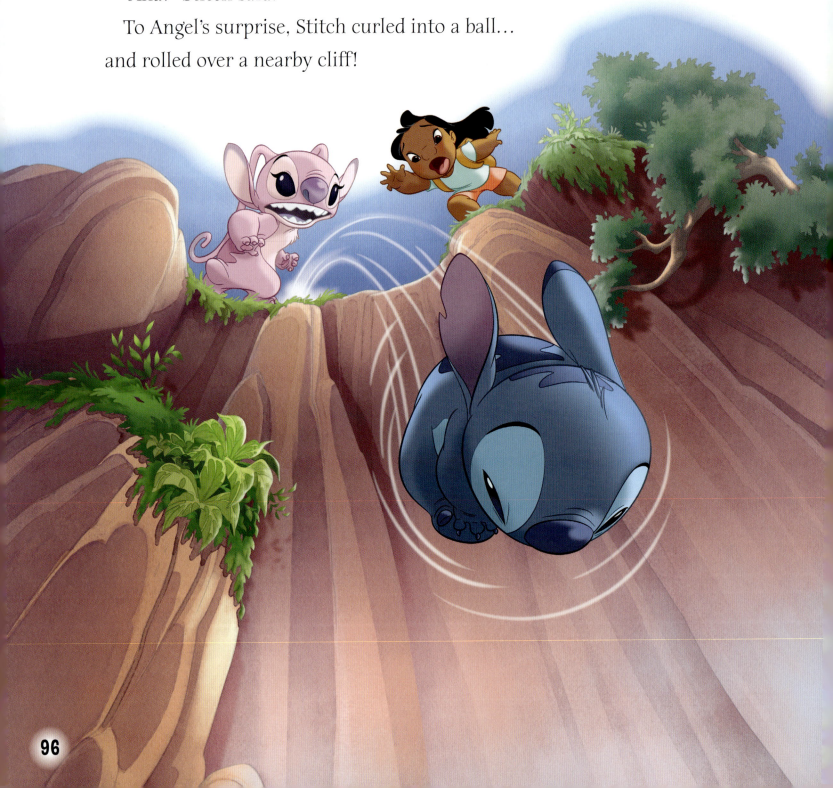

"Aha!" Stitch said.

To Angel's surprise, Stitch curled into a ball…

and rolled over a nearby cliff!

"What's he doing now?" said Lilo.

Angel frowned. She didn't know.

On the beach below, Stitch's two extra arms popped out once more. He raced around the sand, grabbing seashells, palm leaves, driftwood and coconuts.

Then he threw them everywhere. What a mess Stitch was making!

Stitch scrambled back up the cliffside and pointed to the giant heart-shaped message he had created.

Angel squealed with delight. "Valentine?" she asked.

"Valentine," said Stitch.

A Valentine for Stitch

Stitch didn't notice as Lilo pulled a shiny red box out of her backpack.

"I was saving this for you, Stitch. But maybe you should give it to your valentine."

"Chocolate?" asked Stitch.

It looked like he might gobble up the whole thing. Instead, he ripped the box right down the middle!

"Happy Valentine's Day!" said Stitch.

He handed one half of the chocolate box to Angel and the other half to Lilo. Because Stitch didn't have just one valentine. He had two!

STITCH OR TREAT

"Happy Halloween!" Lilo shouted as Stitch entered the kitchen one Saturday morning while Nani, Lilo's sister, made breakfast.

"Halloween?" Stitch asked. He had never heard of Halloween before.

"It's one of my favourite holidays!" Lilo explained. "It's a day where everybody dresses up and eats sweets! Don't worry. I'll tell you everything there is to know!"

"I wrote a checklist for us," Lilo said while Stitch ate his breakfast. She held up a piece of paper. "It has all of the steps we need to complete to have the perfect Halloween."

Lilo explained more as they went up to her bedroom. "First, we need to find you a costume. On Halloween, we get to wear costumes and pretend we're someone or something else, like how I'm a witch." Lilo explained as they went up to her bedroom.

Stitch thought for a second before racing around Lilo's room. He put on a lampshade and a blanket. "Costume?" he asked.

"A Halloween costume should make you feel special," Lilo said. "Does that make you feel special?"

Stitch shook his head.

Stitch or Treat

The pair spent the rest of the morning trying to find the perfect Halloween costume for Stitch.

They attempted one outfit after the next. But no costume fit just right. Finally, they found something that made Stitch feel special!

Lilo and Stitch headed back downstairs. "Now it is time for pumpkin carving!" Lilo proclaimed. "On Halloween, we like to turn pumpkins into jack-o'-lanterns by giving them faces."

With Nani's help, Lilo cut a nose, eyes and mouth into her pumpkin, then showed it to Stitch.

"Now you try!" Lilo said.

Stitch did his best, but his jack-o'-lantern looked a little different from Lilo's.

Still, Lilo clapped her hands. "Great job, Stitch! Why don't you do another one? I have just the pumpkin!"

Stitch or Treat

Lilo led Stitch and Nani outside to a large pumpkin by the porch.

"Okay, Stitch. Try using this." Lilo handed Stitch his blaster. Then she held up her jack-o'-lantern for reference.

Stitch shot lasers at the pumpkin. When he was done, Stitch smiled.

"Wow!" Lilo exclaimed. "That looks amazing!"

Once they had finished carving pumpkins, Nani and her friend David took Lilo and Stitch into town. Every shop window was decorated in honour of the big Halloween celebration taking place. Stitch had never seen the shops look so ghostly!

"We have to work at the convenience shop for an hour, so don't get into trouble, okay?" Nani said.

"We won't!" promised Lilo.

Lilo turned to Stitch with her list. "Now it's time for the best part of Halloween – trick-or-treating!" Lilo exclaimed. "That is where we knock on doors and say 'trick or treat' to get sweets."

"Trick! Trick!" Stitch jumped up and down in excitement.

"Tricks are fun," Lilo said. "But remember, the most important part is the sweets."

As Stitch followed Lilo, he was still thinking about the tricks.

Lilo approached the first shop and knocked.

The shopkeeper opened the door and greeted them with a bowl of delicious-looking sweets.

Lilo held out her bag. "Trick or —"

"TRICK!" Stitch shouted. He jumped in front of Lilo and transformed so
that all six of his limbs waggled wildly!

The shopkeeper shrieked, slammed the door and bolted the lock.

The pair headed to the next shop with their empty sweet bags. "Don't forget the treat part of trick-or-treating, Stitch! Remember, it is more important to get lots of sweets," Lilo said.

Stitch nodded, but something else had caught his eye.

After passing through a crowd, Lilo realised Stitch was gone. "Stitch, where'd you go?!"

Just then, she heard a scream and suspected that Stitch had something to do with it...

Try as he might, Stitch couldn't resist tricking people, and Lilo still hadn't received any sweets at all.

Sighing, Lilo decided she didn't want to trick-or-treat any more.

Once she was alone, Lilo took out her list. She had been so close to having the perfect Halloween. If only Stitch hadn't gone and ruined it with all his mischief!

Now there was no way she would be able to complete her checklist.

Just then, a scary shadow fell across Lilo's path!

But it was only Stitch, standing on a pile of sweets. "Treat?" he offered.

He wanted to fix what he had done and make Halloween truly special for Lilo.

"Stitch! This is amazing!" Lilo cheered. "But how did you get all of these sweets for us?"

Stitch gave her a guilty look.

Back on the main street, Lilo noticed no one else had any sweets.

"Stitch! You can't just trick everyone and steal their sweets! Sweets have to be given!" said Lilo.

"But… perfect Halloween?" he asked.

Stitch or Treat

Lilo knew Stitch had meant well in trying to make her Halloween the best one ever. She also knew they had to make Halloween right for everyone else.

If only they could figure out how...

Just then, Stitch had an idea and raced away.

He returned a few minutes later – with his spaceship! They could use it to drop sweets into people's bags!

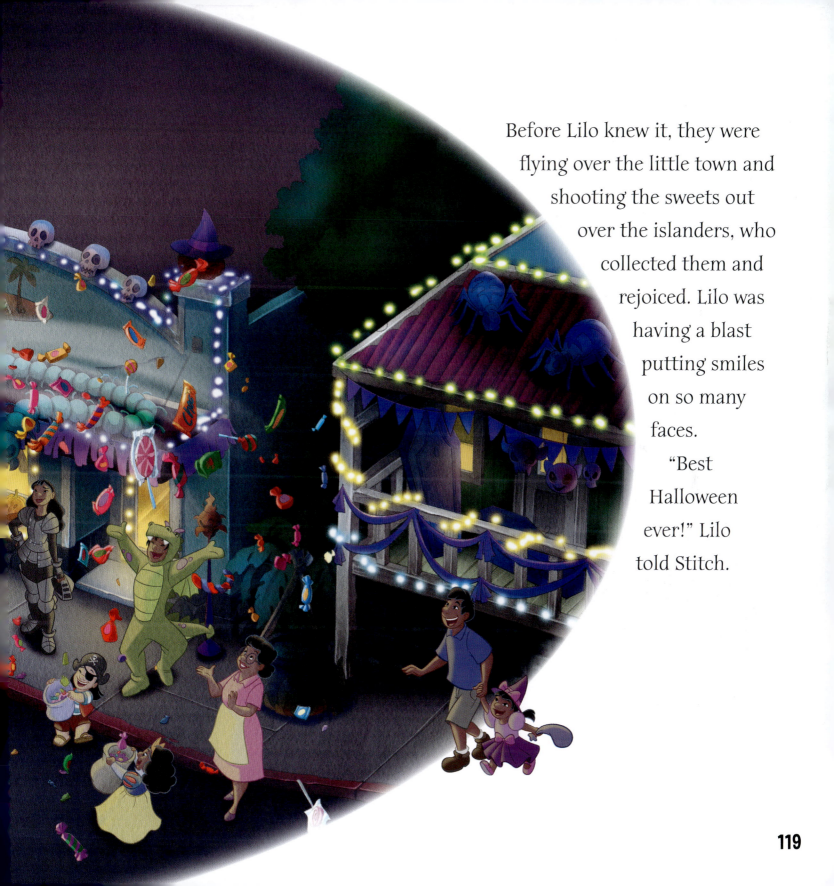

Before Lilo knew it, they were flying over the little town and shooting the sweets out over the islanders, who collected them and rejoiced. Lilo was having a blast putting smiles on so many faces.

"Best Halloween ever!" Lilo told Stitch.

That night, Lilo decided there was no perfect checklist for a fun Halloween. And Stitch learnt that getting to eat lots of sweets was even better than playing tricks.

It really was the best Halloween ever – for everyone.

STITCH'S DAY AT SCHOOL

Lilo and Stitch were excited. It was Pet Day at school, and all the kids were bringing their pets to class.

121

"Hurry up, Lilo!" Nani, Lilo's older sister, called. "You'll be late for school!"

Stitch's Day at School

Nani looked at Stitch. "We're going to be on our best behaviour today, right?"

At school, there were all different kinds of pets. Some were big and fluffy. Some were small and scaly. Some even looked like their owners!

The class also had a pet of their own, a frog named Mr Phibbs. But none of the animals looked like Stitch.

Stitch's Day at School

After each presentation, Lilo got more and more excited. She couldn't wait for her turn.

Stitch was curious about all the different creatures. But when he tried to get a closer look at the class pet...

… Mr Phibbs jumped out of his tank and right out the door!

Stitch chased after
Mr Phibbs. The frog hopped
down the hall and into
another classroom.

In that classroom, students wore goggles and aprons as they worked on experiments. It reminded Stitch of Jumba's lab. Stitch knew he should find Mr Phibbs and get back to Lilo, but he couldn't resist trying his own experiment.

With some careful pours
and shakes, Stitch created
a stink bomb that sent
everyone scrambling
from the room…
including his
froggy friend.

The hallway was filled with students heading towards the cafeteria. How would he ever find Mr Phibbs in that crowd?

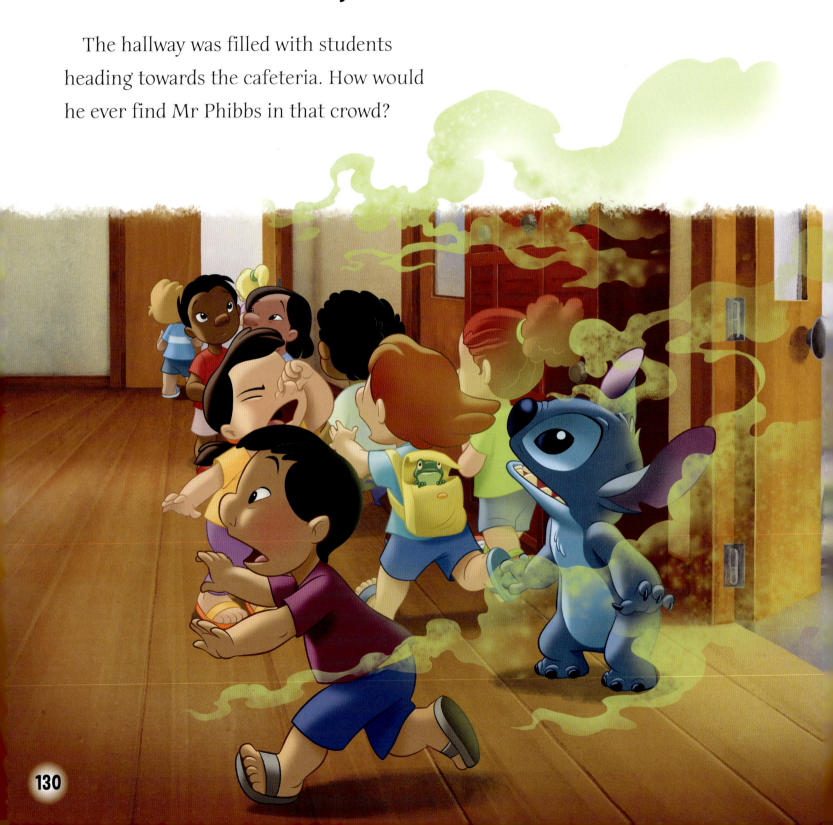

Stitch's Day at School

But Stitch didn't have to worry. Mr Phibbs hopped right by him in the cafeteria. Stitch tried to grab him… but missed.

"Food fight!"

As the cafeteria erupted into chaos, Stitch spotted Mr Phibbs jumping out the door.

Stitch's Day at School

As the frog hopped from room to room, Stitch followed. But every time he got close, something new would catch his eye.

During maths, he remembered what Nani had said about 'best behaviour'. School was interesting, but the clock was ticking and he needed to get back to class with Mr Phibbs… and fast!

At last, Stitch found Mr Phibbs...

Stitch's Day at School

... just as a whistle blew, and red rubber balls filled the air.
Stitch ducked, jumped and cartwheeled across the auditorium...
and caught Mr Phibbs! Now he could get back to class.

And just in time! It was Lilo's turn to introduce her pet for Pet Day. "My name is Lilo Pelekai, and this is Stitch," she said. "He's my... Stitch."

"What an… unusual pet," said
the teacher.

"Yes, ma'am," said Lilo. "That's
because Stitch isn't just a pet.
He's my best friend and part of my
'ohana – and 'ohana means family!"

137

Nani met Lilo and Stitch after school.

"Pet Day was great!" Lilo said. "Stitch was on his best behaviour."

"Really?" Nani asked. "I mean, really? I think that calls for some ice cream."

Stitch agreed. This was the best Pet Day ever!